Northern Ireland & Scotland

Edited By Donna Samworth

First published in Great Britain in 2017 by:

Young Writers
Remus House
Coltsfoot Drive
Peterborough
PE2 9BF
Telephone: 01733 890066
Website: www.youngwriters.co.uk

All Rights Reserved
Book Design by Spencer Hart
© Copyright Contributors 2017
SB ISBN 978-1-78820-494-1
Printed and bound in the UK by BookPrintingUK
Website: www.bookprintinguk.com
YB0330F

FOREWORD

Young Writers is proud to present, 'Welcome To Wonderland – Northern Ireland & Scotland'.

For our latest mini saga competition, we asked secondary school pupils to create a story with a beginning, middle and end, with the added challenge of keeping to 100 words.

The result is this collection of fantastic fiction where our writers invite you in to their whole new worlds. Get ready for an adventure as you discover different dimensions with war and battles, sweet dream lands, disturbing dystopias and never-ending nightmares. From the weird to the wonderful, there is something here to suit everyone.

There was a great response to this competition which is always nice to see, and the standard of entries was excellent, so I'd like to say a big thank you and well done to everyone who entered.

I hope you enjoy reading these mini sagas as much as I did.

Keep writing!

Donna Samworth

CONTENTS

Independent Entries

Clara McNally (15)	1
Eve O'Doherty (12)	2

Carrickfergus College, Carrickfergus

Amy Ross-Wells (13)	3
Jack Davidson (12)	4
Jessica Montgomery (12)	5
Jamie Rodgers (12)	6
Rachael Foster (12)	7
Kristopher Campbell (13)	8
Casey Holmes (13)	9
Tori Susan Broome (13)	10
Bret Bernardino (12)	11
Courtney Cromie (14)	12
Hollie Victoria Stinton (13)	13
Molly McBride (12)	14
Lara Mary Bailey (14)	15
Abbie Martha Anne Thompson (14)	16
Molly Crothers (13)	17
Sophie Jean Thompson (13)	18
Joshua Miller (13)	19
Charlotte Ross (14)	20
Kate Neill (13)	21
Aaron McCalmont (13)	22
Rabeka Mcmurtry (14)	23
Charlie Nicole Louise McGookin (13)	24
Sophie Louise Tourish (12)	25
Aimee Patricia Walker (14)	26
Beth Cairns (15)	27
Kai Aaron Farr (13)	28
Katy Turkington (13)	29
Ben Nicholl (12)	30
Finlay Buchanan (12)	31
Lauren Herron	32
Ethan Scott Gamble (12)	33
Niamh Alexander (13)	34
Gemma Moore (15)	35
Nicholas McCrory (14)	36
Connor McCrum (13)	37

Carrickfergus Grammar School, Carrickfergus

Lara Yorke (12)	38
Ellie Francey (13)	39
Ben Martin (13)	40
Caoimhe Dorrian (11)	41
Kuba Glogowski	42
Amber Nelson (12)	43
Luke Stephenson	44
Daniel Stephen Gardner (13)	45
Charlotte Graham (13)	46
Amy R Bell (13)	47
Thea Nordmann (12)	48
Dylan Gordon (13)	49
Leonardo Evangelista (12)	50
Amy Bell (13)	51
Daniel Hoban (13)	52
Abby Taylor Green (12)	53
Ella Kitchen (12)	54
Alex Philip Newell (14)	55
Yasin Difallah (13)	56
Blake Campbell (13)	57
Anna O'Gara (13)	58
Emili Jayne Irvine (14)	59
Adam Dela Byrne (13)	60

Kyle King (13)	61
Gemma James (12)	62
Mark Norris (13)	63
Kaci Dawson (12)	64
Judith Gregory (13)	65
James McAuley (13)	66
Sacha Irwin (12)	67
Holly Campbell (13)	68
Olivia Smith (13)	69
Erin Gardner (13)	70
Holly Aishling Disley (12)	71
Sophie Purvis (12)	72
Daniel Sharpe (15)	73
Kelsey Blakely (14)	74
Emma Weir	75
Bailey Mcalister (12)	76
Amye Louise Sleator (13)	77
Abi Crooks (12)	78
Robbie Taylor (13)	79
Adam McConnell (12)	80
Sarah Boyd (13)	81
Laura Madden (12)	82
Reece William Stronge (14)	83
Megan Spence (12)	84
Elizabeth Mary Hanna (13)	85
Ryan Kennedy (12)	86
Abbie Clarke	87
Paige Pollock (12)	88
Cameron Long (14)	89
Caitlin MacManus (13)	90
Jay MacQuarrie (13)	91
Madison Abigail Doyle (13)	92
Ruth Sarah McElveen (13)	93
Evan Higgins (12)	94
Asha McClean (12)	95
Sarah Brown	96
Kristen Moore (12)	97
Finlay A Rogan (14)	98
Jake Corbett (12)	99
Lloyd Cole (13)	100
Rhys Pennell (12)	101
Aimee McCartan (13)	102
Grace Delucchi (12)	103
Nicola Smyth (12)	104
Jessica Hayes (12)	105
Reuben Baker	106
Joshua Strudwick (13)	107
Lewis Elmes (14)	108
Alex Millar (12)	109
Lara Ellerslie	110
Jack Campbell (13)	111
Jonathan Geoff Graham (14)	112

Elgin High School, New Elgin

Callum Squair (11)	113
Abbie Howie (11)	114
Alana Marie Wall (12)	115
Jennifer McBride (11)	116
Emillie Dean (12)	117
Eve Campbell (12)	118
Ben Grant (12)	119
Katie Louise Mighten (12)	120
Olivia Eve Ravenscroft (12)	121
Emma-Jayne Russell (12)	122
Kaitlin Duggan (11)	123
Ann-Mairi Stevenson (11)	124
Kian Stanford (12)	125
Cameron Donaldson (12)	126
Amy Leigh Taylor (11)	127
Tyler-James Green (12)	128
Aidan Roger (11)	129
Lauren Davies (11)	130

Mackie Academy, Stonehaven

Ross Allan (13)	131
Molly Brown (12)	132
Cameron Goodall Duncan (13)	133
Jack Beattie (12)	134
Helena Rendall (12)	135
Aaron Henry (12)	136
Abbey Lindsay (13)	137
Ellie Katy Smith (13)	138
Lucy Henry (12)	139
Richie Henderson (13)	140
Marci-Beth Pyper Robertson (12)	141

Samuel William McFarland (13)	142
Cara Davie (12)	143
Mairi Elizabeth Wilson (13)	144
Stuart Burr (13)	145
Nikkitta-Marie Julie Clark (12)	146
Ellen Thomson (12)	147

St Brigid's College, Shantallow

Rebecca-Jane Browne (14)	148
Sarah Ramsey (14)	149
Darren O'Donnell (14)	150
Peter Rodgers (14)	151

Untitled

Heavy. That's the only word I'd use to describe how I felt at that moment. Every heartbeat seems to drag me down further, paralysing me as the man above me presses the cool barrel of his gun to my forehead. His eyes, oh God, his eyes... they pierce me with the strength of a thousand knives, I think I'd rather be stabbed than endure his gaze for a moment longer. 'Oi!' he spits at me, eyeing my tribal tattoo as a look of recognition flashes through his eyes. 'You're the prince...' he spits, before seizing my arm. 'You're coming with me.'

Clara McNally (15)

The Reverse World

Once upon a time, there was a truly awful girl called Ellie. She thought she knew everything but there was one thing she didn't know. She was living in a reverse world. She used to be a perfect child until her and her family moved to the reverse world. Now Ellie was a horrible girl who hated her parents.
One night, she dreamt that she could kill her parents. She hated her parents as she thought they were far to kind and happy. When she tried to kill her parents, it went reverse and her parents killed her!

Eve O'Doherty (12)

Untitled

Smoke, rubble and people panicking, searching for each other, are everywhere. 'What are we going to do?' questions John, looking over at the flames threatening to spread over the rest of the plane.
'I don't know,' whispers Tilly, still in shock.
'Help me get to the pilot's radio,' says Luke.
Luke starts off running before the others can register what he has said. Running, dodging hand luggage that's fallen everywhere. Suddenly, Tilly screams, 'Stop!' Luke turns around and gives her a questioning look. A loud bang is heard and Luke turns around to see the flames have reached the oil tank.

Amy Ross-Wells (13)
Carrickfergus College, Carrickfergus

The Infection

Technology was taking over, when a science branch, called Elemental Hunters, tested a brand new element. During the test it went wrong, creating undead zombies. When Kyle knew about this he told Jamie, 'The zombies are coming.'
'I hope it's not one of your immature pranks,' Jamie replied.
'I'm not joking!' Kyle said in disbelief. So they thought what should they do (for about 2-3 minutes). They decided to defend themselves.
Hours later an evacuation ship came to rescue them from this horrible mess. I wonder where on Earth they took them, at least the two of them were safe.

Jack Davidson (12)
Carrickfergus College, Carrickfergus

WD-467

Completely broken. As I stare out of my bunker I can't comprehend what's happened. Society is out of control. An absolute disaster. Body fat of victims powering the ongoing flames, charred beyond belief. There is nothing left. Who knew one scam would turn into this? A completely destroyed world. Gunshots fired rapidly, wiping out whoever they could. Buildings crumble as the flames shoot at them. Suddenly, I hear a voice, the president. 'Do you think they'll know it was us?' Angry beyond belief, honestly. How was I going to fix this? I must come up with a plan...

Jessica Montgomery (12)
Carrickfergus College, Carrickfergus

Element 155

As the evil spread throughout the land and killed everyone in sight, Rictoven tried to stop them but it was no use. Soon the zombies had killed everyone but two people - Tank and Rictoven. Tank shouted over to him, 'How did this happen?' Rictoven replied, 'I unearthed a new element 155 and we started mining it but we mined into ancient catacombs and the zombies killed all of them!' Tank grabbed a grenade and threw it at all the undead.
Tank yelled, 'This is it, Rictoven, it is the end. We'll be killed by the cursed and undead...'

Jamie Rodgers (12)
Carrickfergus College, Carrickfergus

Magical World

It all started on the 17th February when we were all out for Rachael's birthday party. While everyone was getting photos in the woods, Rachael and Aimee went off to explore. They found a sparkling stone and picked it up. In a flash they were in a different, unreal magical world! They looked around and there was everything they had ever wanted. There were unicorns, money on trees, Lamborghinis, everything. They met some unreal creatures and extraordinary animals - but it all had to come to an end so they said goodbye to all their friends and went back to our world.

Rachael Foster (12)
Carrickfergus College, Carrickfergus

Ruined World

I woke up, my watch beeped 7.30 hours. I got up, put on my uniform and headed down the ruined subway. Sam and Mirabelle were chatting to each other, I approached them. 'Hey Sniffs!' called Mirabelle. I bolted past Sam before he had a chance to start his daily thirty minute talk. I went into our control room, a train yard. 'Rookie, late for yet another briefing.'
'Sorry ma'am, I was resting.'
Half an hour later we split up. Me, Sam and Mirabelle went out into the ruined Manhattan to scavenge supplies to survive this aftermath.

Kristopher Campbell (13)
Carrickfergus College, Carrickfergus

The Volturi Has Risen

Gastonia was a calm place full of supernatural creatures but things changed when the Volturi vampires took control. The Volturi changed my life. I am now one of them. We took control over a decade ago. We are the biggest sire of vampires in the universe. People with potential attract us and we change them. Glastonia is no longer that calm place anymore. It is full of murderous beings. Werewolves, vampires, witches, you name it. Many covens and clans have tried to stop us. They all have failed. Volturi vampires are the strongest in the world. Nothing can stop us.

Casey Holmes (13)
Carrickfergus College, Carrickfergus

Make A Difference

She looked back one last time before her wings spread from her back and she flew away. I'll never see her again. She has gone to rule a different world and show them how to care for their unique planet... Earth, I think it's called. They are the only species left with access to water. We have to get our water from healers; they've learned to turn our smoke-filled world into a similar landscape to Earth. Even though she won't be accepted, she doesn't care. She wants to help them stop destroying the most beautiful thing in the universe.

Tori Susan Broome (13)
Carrickfergus College, Carrickfergus

Untitled

I remember this day like it was yesterday; people crying, running, it all started with four factions: defenders, creators, farmers and crazies. My name is Jon and I'm a defender. My brother is David, he's a crazy, he wants to control everybody and take their freedom. They come and leave warnings. For a day they will come and take freedom.
We were all in our cabins then suddenly skies turned red and clouds turned black. We all could see the crazies carrying their bombs, tanks and bombs. It was a matter of time - I took my life to save.

Bret Bernardino (12)
Carrickfergus College, Carrickfergus

The Others

I awoke to the smell of burning flames, they were surrounding me. 'Where am I?' I mumbled, as I reached for my phone in my back pocket. The date read: 'Friday 13th December 2020'. What is going on? I needed answers, but my vision was bleary. I could see the distorted silhouette of a woman. 'Help!' I shout in despair. She slowly turned around, my heart was racing. As she gradually stumbled towards me I could see this wasn't any woman, this was a horrifying creature. I started to back away from her, but then I saw the others.

Courtney Cromie (14)
Carrickfergus College, Carrickfergus

Soulmate

Two minutes, twenty-four seconds, that's all I have until I meet her. Will she have blue eyes or green? Blonde hair or brown? I don't know. My grandfather told me the legend. 'The numbers counting down on your arm aren't how long you have left to live, no, it's until you meet the one - your soulmate.' I'm running down the street passing all these couples searching for my soulmate. I trip and fall onto someone. I look at my arm and it says: 0.00.00. I take a glance at the woman before me, we both say, 'It's you.'

Hollie Victoria Stinton
Carrickfergus College, Carrickfergus

Frost Mountains

In the world of Taurolia, near the scorched mountains of Pangea, lives an Argalai called Orion. Normally, the weather is around 165 degrees, which Argalais love, as it removes excess moisture from their bodies. But Orion noticed something. An ice mountain! There hadn't been a trace of water around here ever, much less ice! Orion needed to act fast. He needed to get to the council fast, so he started his journey. He got there fast but they had been evacuated. When he got closer, he realised they were going deep underground to escape definite doom!

Molly McBride (12)
Carrickfergus College, Carrickfergus

Nightmares

My sister got really sick, it took over her brain and the doctors didn't know what to do. That was until the experimental drug! I was the first to volunteer for it to be tested on. That's how I got struck here, in my own brain, trust me it's terrible, every dream, every nightmare and every experience lives here and I can't get out. When I was little my parents died. My mistake will haunt me forever. No, I didn't kill my parents, but I'll tell you later on, well it actually happen- 'No, no, get away, let me go!'

Lara Mary Bailey (14)
Carrickfergus College, Carrickfergus

Ready To Go

It's 3017. Earth just isn't right anymore. Breathing is the only thing I haven't forgotten how to do. Some can't even do that anymore without a bomb or a bullet stopping them. I'm old now and can't even leave my house without seeing someone get killed. I've refused to eat and drink for days, there's just no point anymore. All I have left to offer is kindness; I can't stop this war, although I wish I could. I can feel my body shutting down and I'm ready. But I was kind. I hope one day that will be enough.

Abbie Martha Anne Thompson (14)
Carrickfergus College, Carrickfergus

Gateway To Darkness

It was dark and black, everything was invisible. Howling came from afar, he was scared, he was lonely, he was the man to enter a whole new universe. Suddenly, he remembered he had a flashlight that he picked up to see what the funny noise was. Moments later, he felt a brisk breath on his fingers and looked down to find six wolves staring at him. He became fond of them and he noticed them trying to lead him back. They reached a glowing red portal and tried walking through but it closed and disappeared. Whispers of ghosts, demonising ghosts...

Molly Crothers (13)
Carrickfergus College, Carrickfergus

Eclipsus

Once, there was a distant realm not so different from our own, in this world there lived a young woman called Sapphire, she was a very talented person, the only problem was that she was a girl and her society disagreed with females doing the same as males. Sapphire was very good at science, and also very good with computers.

One day she discovered a magic charm with a picture of a total solar eclipse on it. When she touched the image it started glowing and getting bigger until it was the size of a door, it was really spectacular.

Sophie Jean Thompson (13)
Carrickfergus College, Carrickfergus

The Legend Of Kalakutam

Once, there was a fairly peculiar land known as Kalakutam. It was once a place where the oddest thing was normal, maybe that is why they didn't see the horrific day when it all changed. For what they knew it was just another day in the uncommon world. They didn't suspect anything, not even the magnificent oracles saw it coming. Unfortunately, there was one that used his power for darkness. This empty soul went by the name of Abigor. They saw him as a saviour, though he was an empty man. His vacant soul would bring end to the realms.

Joshua Miller (13)
Carrickfergus College, Carrickfergus

Perfect Until...

I have always loved life, especially since Michelle Obama became president. We all have equal rights, there is no war and over the years humans have adapted to a peaceful life. There is no litter or poverty, rich or poor people, no one is better than anyone and everyone is equal and different in their own ways. My life has been perfect from when I open my eyes until I close my eyes and when I look outside it always looks the exact same perfect way with the trees swaying in the same direction, the birds chirping. Until one day...

Charlotte Ross (14)
Carrickfergus College, Carrickfergus

Air-Raid Shelter Portal

There I was, hiding in an air raid shelter, hiding for my life, I was surrounded by like, twenty other people, we were all sitting in fear. You could hear them dropping bombs. Every time it sounded like it was getting closer and closer. You could hear people crying and screaming. Then, out of nowhere, a bomb dropped. Just behind our air raid shelter, it made lots of noise, loads of people ran out to see. There was a massive hole in the ground, but it was glowing purple, people started to jump in and then I jumped in after them.

Kate Neill (13)
Carrickfergus College, Carrickfergus

Impossible

I remember when I heard the creak from my bedroom door and arose above the end of my bed. It was green, slimy and lizard-like with a long tail. It snatched me before I could shout help and jumped out my window with me. It threw me on the ship and took off to what they call Zarlex. I remember landing and getting out to tonnes of the creatures cheering and hissing. I was forced to build houses for them with other kids. I asked, 'How long until we leave this place?'
'You will never leave. It is impossible.'

Aaron McCalmont (13)
Carrickfergus College, Carrickfergus

Final Breath

I heard the explosions in the distance, clearly another life lost or many! I sat on top of the apartment complex with my legs dangling over the edge. They were coming for me next, I could hear them running up the stairs, nuclear war is worse than they said, no amount of preparation could get you ready for this, they're here now, the psychotic mutants. I take one last breath before I push myself over. Soon I will be out of this awful world. I'm falling so fast and it's the most free I've felt in a very long time...

Rabeka Mcmurtry (14)
Carrickfergus College, Carrickfergus

Elliopia

There were thousands of portals opening and closing. I missed every single one. '16th June 7004, dear Diary, I have been searching tirelessly and I found some sort of white gun. It had purple glowing liquid inside. I don't know what it is but I'm going for it. Yours sincerely, Mia'. With a bang, I shot it at my feet. I arrived in a futuristic land, magical plants everywhere. In the distance I could make out a human, it got closer. It got bigger, it looked like a girl. She had long locks of hair down her back.

Charlie Nicole Louise McGookin (13)
Carrickfergus College, Carrickfergus

Atticpia

Miss sent me to the attic to get books. I forgot which one. I picked up one called 'Atticpia'. All of a sudden the door opened. I stepped inside. I was scared. Within an instant I was in line with a bunch of goblins. I was handed a nettle gun that said: 'Dusty, rule Atticpia'. Next thing I knew I had wings and was lifting off the ground toward some clean goblins. There were stingy nettles coming from everywhere. Then there was black. Had I fainted? When I woke up a doctor told me I had. But I'm sure I didn't.

Sophie Louise Tourish (12)
Carrickfergus College, Carrickfergus

The Mysterious Killer

I woke up with pains in my head, shooting like daggers! I look around and realise I'm no longer at home. I see a dirty room. I try raising my hands to my head as my vision goes blurry. My arms are restrained by something. I look around and see something with horns and blue skin staring at me! Then something flashes in its hand. It walks closer and I realise it's carrying a sword! 'No!' I scream, and plea for mercy. He just lets out a deep laugh, raises the sword and slams it viciously down into my chest!

Aimee Patricia Walker (14)
Carrickfergus College, Carrickfergus

Untitled

I awoke in my dark room to find I was alone. I opened my curtains to the cold, empty world, left scared by the war, leaving me alone. There had been no birds to keep me company, nor to fill the ever long silence, all other life had died in the war. They said, 'Right time, right place.' Well, for me that was the horrific truth, I was alone in the right place, right time. I went out to find some food. Once I returned I found the door... open, I cautiously entered thinking... *I had closed that door.*

Beth Cairns (15)
Carrickfergus College, Carrickfergus

The Black City

There is an evil city, called the Black City, where it is dark all the time. There is a small boy called Jeff, who has made a plan to escape. Jeff grabbed his bag and was ready to go but when he leaves that dark, evil door there's no going back. Jeff ran out the door, dodging criminals who were trying to kill him. He runs into a dead end of an alley with criminals walking towards him with all sorts of weapons. He knows it's over. That's when he remembers the saying 'No one escapes the Black City alive'.

Kai Aaron Farr (13)
Carrickfergus College, Carrickfergus

A Step Beyond

Feeling the scorching sun on my face, I opened my eyes and all I saw was desert. Where on Earth was I? The last thing I remembered was stepping off the footpath outside my house. Suddenly, I heard terrifying roars and the Earth started to tremble. Shielding my eyes, I saw a sand storm in the distance coming towards me at lightning speed. Unbelievably, two dinosaurs were fighting ferociously. Where am I? What year is it? In a blind panic, I started to run. Suddenly I was back on the footpath. Really... did I just time travel?

Katy Turkington (13)
Carrickfergus College, Carrickfergus

Wonder World

One day there was a boy called George, he moved house to a place called Coolpool. He met a friend, called Geoff, and they went to explore the estate. There was a large hill with lots of trees, they went into the trees and found a hidden temple with a portal. They stepped inside the portal and they were shocked when they entered the portal. There was lots and lots of tall trees with very small people. They loved to climb the tall trees. The boys went to explore the world, they came across a lake which was really clean.

Ben Nicholl (12)
Carrickfergus College, Carrickfergus

Paradise We Think

One scorching hot day, a family got stranded on an island with nobody else on the island. They were visiting the beautiful island when the boat left them behind. They have to look for food and also they have to stock up on food, so that in emergencies there is food on hand. They are also unable to buy medication so they have to make their own medicine. Will they ever get back home? Will they ever see humans ever again? Guess we will have to wait and see if they will ever see their lovely family again.

Finlay Buchanan (12)
Carrickfergus College, Carrickfergus

Enchanted Forest

It all started with going to bed but when I woke, I was in an enchanted forest, so I got up and started to walk about. The ground felt weird on my feet, the trees were all different colours and it was like the plants were alive and could move about. I was so scared, it was like someone put virtual reality goggles on me but suddenly this weird monkey-looking thing ran up to me and gave me an electric shock! Then I really woke up and realised it was my phone vibrating and thankfully it was only a dream!

Lauren Herron
Carrickfergus College, Carrickfergus

Hell Land

Once upon a time there was no Earth, it was just a ball of fire. Demons came down from hell to take all parents.
One day, two boys and one girl were going to stand up to all these demons and their leader, Borgz. So they set off to the demon's world to set the parents free. When they got there they realised that there were lots of guards so they had to climb up the wall, but when they got to the top, Borgz was there, so, they pushed him off the demon castle, into the fire pits.

Ethan Scott Gamble (12)
Carrickfergus College, Carrickfergus

The Monkey's Adventure

One day a monkey, called Steve, and his family moved to a place called New Town. It was a new jungle with lots of trees, well that's what monkeys like. When they just moved Steve got lost, he didn't know what to do so he went everywhere to try and find his family but he couldn't find them. He went and asked all these different animals if they had seen his family but they said no. Poor Steve was really scared but in a few minutes someone called, it was his family. Steve was so happy.

Niamh Alexander (13)
Carrickfergus College, Carrickfergus

A Forgotten Memory

We have come far in this world of ours, well, considering the damage that has been done... it's an improvement. I remember how the pond by our house used to sparkle like the stars on a starry night and now and then you looked deep down into it, you could see every freckle that was on your face, as your reflection was as clear as a blue sky on a summer's day. Among the laughs and the long summer days and nights by the pond, this is all just a forgotten memory.

Gemma Moore (15)
Carrickfergus College, Carrickfergus

The Two Stones

What have they done? All they had to do was leave the damn stone alone. I told them messing with time had drastic consequences but they had to do the one thing I told them not to. Now the damage they have done is irreversible, time itself is falling apart. At least KFC still exists in the future. I destroyed the universe - what a great name - destroyer of the universe. I could have stopped it. I'm confused on how I'm alive and what does that other stone do...

Nicholas McCrory (14)
Carrickfergus College, Carrickfergus

Welcome To Wonderland

I walk into the battlefield, scared of what might happen to me. I live on Earth, it's 2117 and I am fighting for my country. Humans are in need of resources but other planets are keeping them for themselves. I'm not the only one on the battlefield; there are robots helping us fight. Only hope can save Planet Earth now before it's too late.

Connor McCrum (13)
Carrickfergus College, Carrickfergus

Unwelcome Guest

'Today's the day, Aditina! Time to get up!' King Zimbab arrived in her room enthusiastically. The king was going away on a trip to sort out trades and Aditina, Zimbab's eldest child out of fourteen, was due to reign as queen until he got back. Zimbab left and Aditina got to work. 'So what's first?' she giggled, 'oh, sighing forms, that's boring!' 'That's what's to be done, Aditina!' the advisor claimed. 'Very well.'

While she was reading forms, she was getting scared, every paper read, 'It's coming, get out!' It was quite frightening. Then... suddenly something burst in the doors!

Lara Yorke (12)
Carrickfergus Grammar School, Carrickfergus

Underground Mania Nearly Caught

'Jaxx, get up it's time to go,' shouted his mum, Amy.
'Coming!'
It was Jaxx's first day on the guarding job.
Una arrived at the door. 'Is Jaxx ready?' asked Una, then Jaxx came running down the stairs and they set off.
'Ready? Your ears might pop,' laughed Una. *Bang! Pop!*
The flying car was off to the people's home on the surface.
Una was a fairy and she could turn into a figure. 'Oh no!' exclaimed Una. 'A human!'
A child picked Una up and cried 'Look Mummy a flying car and a fairy.'
Oh no, better call the Captain, thought Una...

Ellie Francey (13)
Carrickfergus Grammar School, Carrickfergus

Arthur's Stone

'I can't believe this!' Arthur exclaimed, worrying. 'Why are we here?' Exactly three minutes ago, Arthur and I were in an abandoned mansion wandering aimlessly around looking for something valuable. Arthur found a gem which teleported us to a parallel world when we touched it. This parallel world was filled with corpses, ruling and moving about like nothing had happened.
'What is that up there?' I questioned Arthur. 'Whatever that glistening thing is, it's probably worthless.'
'But it shines like the sun for this land, it's beau... ' After a piercing pain in my shoulder, we were now the living dead!

Ben Martin (13)
Carrickfergus Grammar School, Carrickfergus

The Mysterious Night

'It sounds so silent up there,' Sarah stutters.
'We will go up there now,' Nathan demanded. *Squeak! Creak! Bang! Boom!*
Nathan bravely opens the door to the rusty, dark storm shelter as Sarah follows behind.
'Wow, this place is trashed!' Sarah exclaims loudly. The whole town was trashed, windows smashed, street lights broken, even tiny fires inside shops etc.
'Let's look around, maybe we might find someone to help us,'
Nathan whispered. Sarah found a piece of paper, it was partly ripped but you could still make out some writing. The piece of paper said: 'Beware, as you are next!'

Caoimhe Dorrian (11)
Carrickfergus Grammar School, Carrickfergus

The Galactic Rule Of Tyra

After the galactic government took over Tyra, the residents, called Mools, were enraged. The beautiful nature around them was replaced with dull buildings. The blue grass vanished with only bland, grey roads left. The government also brought along other disrespectful species (especially humans). After 50 years of telling the government to stop, they finally had enough. The galactic government will soon learn that the vicious Mools aren't to be pushed around. The Mools started conquering small, powerless villages before moving on to giant cities. The Mools swarmed the capital, like ants, and the galactic government retreated... or so they thought...

Kuba Glogowski
Carrickfergus Grammar School, Carrickfergus

Demon's Den...!

Crack, crack, crack, went the ancient door to the large haunted castle. The girl stammered, 'Wh-who's th-there?' She tiptoed along corridor, that was as long as forty thousand great whites lined up, as if they were waiting to snap at a fish. She crept up the tornado staircase, she backed away. The fright on her face was unbelievable! She then claimed, 'I-I'm not afraid of you!'
A voice from behind growled, 'Well you should be!'
The doors locked. She tried the window, it disappeared. She was trapped. Forever? Days? Months? Years? She was petrified!
'Are you frightened of me yet...?'

Amber Nelson (12)
Carrickfergus Grammar School, Carrickfergus

The Revenge For Platooney

Platooney. A place that was once popular by its peace, which is now corrupted.
Corrupted by a leader that is vengeful, vengeful for his people!
'Luke, are you awake?' asked Tom.
'What is it?' said Luke tiredly.
'I think they're coming, they're here!' We ran to sound the alarms. Luke and Tom sprinted to the base where they were all ready with their neon-blasters. We heard gunfire, in addition multiple bombs. They saw hundreds of soldiers rush from the base. 'Release the animals!' exclaimed the king. For once there was silence, who knows when they will be back.
'Silence!'

Luke Stephenson
Carrickfergus Grammar School, Carrickfergus

The Future

The rules of the planet are simple - everyone works and makes enough money so they can live and provide for their families. Everyone gets paid enough to live and don't get paid millions for doing their job. But then there was an attack on the rulers, as they were exposed for controlling people and killing anyone who had disobeyed them. This started a war between the rulers and the people. After a long battle, the people finally won. There were lots of casualties on both sides and everyone suffered. Eventually the economy went back to the way it used to be.

Daniel Stephen Gardner (13)
Carrickfergus Grammar School, Carrickfergus

Destruction

Samantha and Sophie were both swimming along the dark depths of their home ocean, everything seemed normal until they made their way into Ocean City. 'Something seems different,' said Samantha. As soon as she finished her sentence she heard loud screams coming from every direction. One of the screams started growing closer and closer. It turned out to be Dale.
'You need to get out of here now, the city is getting destroyed,' said Dale.
'Why? What have we done wrong?' asked Sophie.
'Nothing, our beliefs are what seems to be making them angry.'
They all heard an explosion and...

Charlotte Graham (13)
Carrickfergus Grammar School, Carrickfergus

I Have A Feeling That This Is Not Mars...

All of a sudden, our spacecraft's speed built up, now flying faster than the speed of light.
'I can't control it!' yelled the pilot, pushing all the buttons frantically. *Crash!*
We stayed in our seats for the whole of two minutes, motionless and silent.
You could've cut the atmosphere with a knife. 'I have a feeling that this is not Mars,' I squeaked, breaking the uncomfortable silence. We stood up, our legs numb from the long journey, and opened the metal door... A blast of humid air and the smell of tropical flowers hit us.
'Wow!' I breathed in awe.

Amy R Bell (13)
Carrickfergus Grammar School, Carrickfergus

A Different World

Aqualandia, an underwater world just like ours. Only, one day, a man from above the water comes catapulting into the surrounding bubble. Suddenly, this man is in a strange world. He's looking round with a face full of curiosity. He hasn't registered the hundreds of people staring straight at him...

Like a flash of lightning, people who looked like the police, were sweeping the man up! He's been captured. Many questions are being asked. The man's face is expressionless.

Years have gone by. The man's now joyful and ecstatic. He's adopted this land as his home. He's never seen again...

Thea Nordmann (12)
Carrickfergus Grammar School, Carrickfergus

The Great Quake

'Dylan! Dylan! Get up!' I opened my eyes, the world was spinning and my ears were ringing. I opened my eyes, there was nothing left of the three-storey building I was staying in.Callum was pulling me to my feet. 'Hurry up, they are getting closer.' We were getting hunted down by bandits. 'We only have twenty minutes to make it to the boat!' 'What's happening?' I yelled.
'There was a huge earthquake,' Callum replied.
We were now sprinting through the streets and we could hear the voices of the soldiers on the boat. We had to jump... 'Help!'

Dylan Gordon (13)
Carrickfergus Grammar School, Carrickfergus

Sparcia

We made it to the unknown planet that we've never discovered before. It was dark and dull, nothing was living on the strange planet. 'Look over there!' There was a bright blue structure that exactly fitted a human and one that's... for giants!
We didn't know what to do, everyone was scared and confused. I bravely volunteered. I walked in slowly... *Swoosh!* I got sucked into some sort of teleportation. I landed on a white cloud. I met these intelligent, strong, improved humans who mixed their race with others to make new species. I decided to be part of the Sparcia.

Leonardo Evangelista (12)
Carrickfergus Grammar School, Carrickfergus

What If The World Ended In Two Days...

Dark, darker, the sun's light was climbing. July 3rd. How can it be dark at 10am in summer? It isn't normal. Dying... everything was dying. Animals, plants, everything. July 4th, pitch-blackness. As the day grew the TV went live. 'Breaking news.' According to satellites the sun will continue to lose light until there is nothing... and then a bang... an explosion... everything, everyone you ever knew... gone! This was going to be the last day of existence, there was no way of changing it. Everyone, everywhere, saying goodbye... And just as announced, July 5th 2017, the sun exploded...

Amy Bell (13)
Carrickfergus Grammar School, Carrickfergus

Shattered Realities

Kyrian woke to the sound of his mother's screech piercing the silence. Immediately, he sat up and processed what happened, his heart almost pounding out of his chest. He rushed down the stairs, his mind racing but his body seemed rather uncooperative, he finally reached the kitchen. He saw the sword coated in crimson first, which had pierced his mother's chest, his tears wouldn't stop, he was powerless to help. She was gone... He noticed a letter in her cold, dead hands unfinished, but only two words stood out to him 'Roseblood Pack'. He decided he would leave his village.

Daniel Hoban (13)
Carrickfergus Grammar School, Carrickfergus

The World Under The Waves

The world under the waves is unknown to all kind up above, until one day Clara Mill is surfing and falls underwater. The gloomy depths, soon discovered! Clara is speechless at the mysterious, marvellous and mystical world under the waves. Suddenly a mermaid, with a fluorescent tail, swivels around a rock and approaches Clara, her name is Queen Irina! Many creatures welcome Clara and tell her about the world. Apparently they are planning an attack against Willow City, Clara offers to help. The Irinians daringly defeat the Willites and Clara is the only human to ever visit this extraordinary world!

Abby Taylor Green (12)
Carrickfergus Grammar School, Carrickfergus

Colourmania?

The mysterious door gave a loud creak as I peered inside. I closed the door behind and sharply looked up. Vivid neon flowers were covered in colour. I walked through the brightly coloured, vivid houses and everyone was jumping and dancing. 'Where am I?' I whispered under my breath. I did more investigating of the paint-splattered town. 'Welcome to Colourmania. What is this place?' I looked at my pale skin but it suddenly turned pink. I strolled along the movie-like beach and stared up into the deep purple water.
'Ella! Wake up!' My mind switched to reality.

Ella Kitchen (12)
Carrickfergus Grammar School, Carrickfergus

The Struggle For Power

On the rustic world of Kelewan, where the proud Kelewanese Empire dominated entirely. The Kelewanese are people are ruled by tribes and are mainly poor and lack metals. Kelewan itself is a dry, arid world with many valleys and seas are a scarcity. The most powerful clan was the Thuril who are eternally locked in combat with the Tsurani clan. Now the Thuril hordes lined up, splendid in their wooden armour with magnificent blue plumes, ready to charge against the Tsurani's green-plumed blockade on the opposite side of the valley. With an inhuman roar, the carnage begins...

Alex Philip Newell (14)
Carrickfergus Grammar School, Carrickfergus

War...

Gunfire, explosions and screaming. In this world these are the birds tweets that wake us up in the morning, the sound of our alarm clocks, the way of life works... In this society there are four groups: Civilians, the Resistance, reality warpers and the government. The government are using the innocents for their dirty work and their ultimate goal... world domination! The only people standing in their way are the Resistance, with a little help from some kind reality warpers. With their help, the Resistance might make some new allies or some deadly enemies. In this world life is a gamble...

Yasin Difallah (13)
Carrickfergus Grammar School, Carrickfergus

Big Trouble, Little England

Today was cold, colder than yesterday which was a surprise. Rudolph Hitler, aka Hitler's grandson, was leading the world in a so called 'fabulous' dictatorship. Every country's ruler could bend to his will if he wished. Although there was this nagging thought at the back of his mind about a resistance but he dismissed it as he arrived at the grand Reich in his limousine.

'Danke,' Rudolph said to the driver, then opened his door and walked to the marble building his grandad fought for so long ago in the Second World War.

Today he would make great history.

Blake Campbell (13)
Carrickfergus Grammar School, Carrickfergus

Through The Picture Frame

'Hurry up Julie, we're going to be late!' shouted Julie's dad.
'But Dad, it's only four o'clock, I'm meant to be there by six,' Julie answered.
'But in Heinemann it's 5.50 mactogons.'
Julie was running down the stairs with her suitcase thumping against the steps. She jumped in the car and when they pulled up she saw a raggedy old shop. They went in and Julie watched her dad tap his wand on the picture frame in various places. The picture opened up and he told her to go through and buy a dragon and a ticket for the bus!

Anna O'Gara (13)
Carrickfergus Grammar School, Carrickfergus

The Peaceful Valley

I tremble and smile at the same time. It's so peaceful, the sun beats down on my face as I look around. Suddenly I hear loud, banging footsteps, I search the area to see where it's coming from. Finally coming through the mountain of flowers is a horse with a shadowy figure on top. As it draws nearer I now see a person, she yells, 'Why are you here?' I stand stiff as she gets off the horse beside me. 'Well done!' she mumbles. 'The portal has closed!' she cries.
'What's wrong?' I gasp.
'We're stuck here forever now...'

Emili Jayne Irvine (14)
Carrickfergus Grammar School, Carrickfergus

Breaches

Bleep! Bleep! Bleep! 'Shut that thing off, Gen!' Price shouted.
'Done!' Tomas exclaimed.
'What set off the sensors, Gen?' Price asked.
'I recommend that you send a team down there because that was the Keter sector.'
Price got on the radio and talked a bit then left the room. In the briefing room, he filled in the squad and they got combat ready and left for Keter.
Once down there, they scouted the area looking for anything... like a bomb. The bomb was found and a five-second timer. The Keter programmes would escape!

Adam Dela Byrne (13)
Carrickfergus Grammar School, Carrickfergus

Footmania

There I was next in the line at the border of Footmania, the place where every footballer wanted to be. Three hours later I was there, stepping off the ultrasonic rocket onto the soft, green grass of the planet. I looked across and the wonderful sight of football shops, pitches, stadiums and museums greeted me. I was handed a pair of advanced technology binoculars. I looked through them and saw all the different cultural cities with their own style of stadiums, including Chinese, Australian, Canadian and so many more. This was an exceptional place. This was the planet, Footmania.

Kyle King (13)
Carrickfergus Grammar School, Carrickfergus

Princess Dream

It was dreadful. Grandma Morgathea was gone forever. Her famous aqua necklace was set free to the sea. Princess Ava was not only her grand-daughter but also her best friend. A month later, Princess Ava went down to the Panikkan Sea. It was her in the sea. She talked, she walked towards Ava.

Ava was startled but she began walking closer to Grandma Morgathea, she hugged her, kissed her on the head. It was all so real. Back forever the Panikkan sea-horses, dolphins and fish were laying like pancakes. It was mesmerising, unforgettable. But it was all just an unimaginable dream.

Gemma James (12)
Carrickfergus Grammar School, Carrickfergus

Haunted Mansion

'Let's go,' exclaimed Blake.
'Just a minute,' protested Tom. These were the two boys going on an adventure to see the sight behind the doors of a haunted castle. They arrived in the garden at about 11.55pm and started to walk around to explore. The bell struck at midnight and gave the boys a shock. They saw graves starting to move about. They couldn't believe their eyes when people started to rise from the graves. They ran for their lives straight to the doors of the haunted castle. They quickly opened the door and shut it again. They were trapped..

Mark Norris (13)
Carrickfergus Grammar School, Carrickfergus

Cloudville

It was a normal day in Cloudville, the fish were having a lovely day in the sun. Little did they know something dark and dangerous lurked in the background. After having some fish flakes for lunch, everyone went out to play again, when suddenly they heard a large bang! Everyone stopped and glared in silence. Unexpectedly, a massive swordfish came bolting through the town destroying everything in it's path including the fish. Nearly everyone died in this horrific attack. All except one, the electric blue fish who now sits lonely. Remembering what had happened to his fish friends.

Kaci Dawson (12)
Carrickfergus Grammar School, Carrickfergus

The Crash

I peered anxiously at the clock. The sun gleamed making the sea shimmer like a chandelier. Tia's never late when meeting up. I tore my gaze from the clock to the TV beckoning me... *blip*. Staring in disbelief at the scene on the screen. A wave of shock settled over me then the panic seeped in. Tia's car. Beaten. Obliterated. Crashed. Completely. Time ceased. My surroundings turned to dust. I only focused on that screen. Then I blacked out. All I remember clearly for sure is the sickening smile plastered over my mum's face when she saw that wrecked car.

Judith Gregory (13)
Carrickfergus Grammar School, Carrickfergus

A Disaster Of Proportions

The world was falling apart. Buildings were crumbling, the ground was cracking. Everybody was panicking. For it was the end of the planet Proportions. The Alien mothers were panicking, shouting for their babies. Me? I was sitting with my friends, watching in horror as our planet was destroyed, the only home we had ever known. The spaceship suddenly initiated hyperdrive, which took us to another dimension, where we saw that Proportions was not destroyed, but it was called Earth. We seemed to be drifting towards the planet. We landed and then we got out. But then I was woken up!

James McAuley (13)
Carrickfergus Grammar School, Carrickfergus

Painted In Red

The lights flickered violently. 'Wonderland?' The W was hanging by a few wires and the rest of the letters were slightly crooked. The dark trees loomed above, leaves turned to ashes as they fell like snow to the rubble below. The trees stood high letting shadows cascade to the floor. A creature emerged from the forest and stood below the sign, as the ash fell around it. The creature represented the form of a stag, its face was unnerving, painted white with intricate red designs. It had two holes for unblinking eyes and a wide sinister smile, painted in red.

Sacha Irwin (12)
Carrickfergus Grammar School, Carrickfergus

Running

Running. We're always running from our awful lives. Since Hitler won the war life is hell, all that was good is now evil, expression killed, freedom caged, our livelihoods crushed. Running from a world that doesn't want us, a world that will kill us. Excluded from our world, all we know about the world is the stories we hear from people who remember the old world. If we don't know about the world around us we won't fight for it and what you could have...
'Leave, we must leave now!' they screamed.
'Why? Where can we go?' I whispered.

Holly Campbell (13)
Carrickfergus Grammar School, Carrickfergus

As Her Crown Falls

I prised open the palace doors. I wasn't prepared for the ruin I was soon to witness. It had never occurred to me how naive I was to the adversities of my own country. Corpses lay abandoned of those who only wished to protect others. The sun shed no light on the disfigured buildings that once stood proud. Although my mind struggled to process these thoughts, one other thought haunted my brain. Where was he? I was overwhelmed with uncertainty about whether he was alive. He cared for others more than himself. He couldn't be gone. Not now. Not ever.

Olivia Smith (13)
Carrickfergus Grammar School, Carrickfergus

The Unknown Darkness

The sun reflected on the ground beneath the trees. Fireflies lit up the world like lanterns as the sun disappeared beneath the horizon. The smell of spring started to dissolve through the air. As the night fell, darkness came over the world. The universe seemed to collapse around us. The world appeared to be sleeping. But little did anyone know creatures of darkness and evil woke up. Sounds of silence filled the atmosphere as these creatures awoke. They roamed the Earth, going from house to house each night, trying to find strong humans worthy of being one of them.

Erin Gardner (13)
Carrickfergus Grammar School, Carrickfergus

When Darkness Falls

Charlie's head was full of thoughts. She'd been preparing for this her whole life, and yet didn't feel ready to fight her friends. The blow of a horn and she was off, on her first day of war. Blasters and spaceships flew all around her as she fired her own. It was impossible to see anything in the light, aside from the trolls, that is, before she could pull her trigger once more. Something yanked her hair back, she swung around, *crunch!* Charlie glanced down solemnly at the end of the bloody spear that had pierced her armour... Darkness fell...

Holly Aishling Disley (12)
Carrickfergus Grammar School, Carrickfergus

Cloud Paradise

Swoosh! I'd been swept off my feet and a mixture of emotions were rushing through me! I felt as if I was experiencing the most accurate time travel made yet, although I was in fact floating on a cloud! I landed on the most heavenly and luxurious place you could think of. I was in Cloud World! My imagination was lighting up as if everything I was thinking of had come to life. This place was filled with clouds and a satisfying sunset. There were cloud animals roaming the world. 'Argh!' I was falling rapidly. 'Oh no! Back to reality...'

Sophie Purvis (12)
Carrickfergus Grammar School, Carrickfergus

Fractured

Water shapes the earth we stand on, changes the scent of the air we breathe, douses the primal fire in our souls. Water conquered our world, destroying cities, society and our species' future. We are the human race, the survivors of *the Collapse*. Our forefathers built our island as a utopia and refuge, a symbol of human prosperity. The laws we abide by prohibit us from leaving the island. We are the oppressed and the future. We're shielded, the concrete at our feet triumphs over our old foe. Survival divides, we mend the authoritarian fracture.

Daniel Sharpe (15)
Carrickfergus Grammar School, Carrickfergus

Take It Back

Run! They're coming! The war, the nuclear war, it killed everyone... Well mostly everyone. Those who are left are either dying or they are killing, they will lose their humanity and become one of them...

That is why we have been sent, to stop Shanta from being destroyed. You can't change the past but you can try and save the future. That's what I keep telling myself. The babies, I'm sorry. Growing them in tubes and injecting them with fluid hoping for a vaccine. I would take it back if I could, I'm sorry. Secrets come out in the end...

Kelsey Blakely (14)
Carrickfergus Grammar School, Carrickfergus

Anachronistic

'Argh!' Hannah screamed. Bronwyn and I turned around and spotted a hole in the ground but no sign of Hannah! As we moved closer to the hole we were sucked down through it into the past - 1817! 'Help!' We heard Hannah screaming and saw a man in Victorian clothes dragging her! We dashed over and grabbed Hannah's hand but weren't quick enough as we became captured in the back of his cart. We screamed all the way until he stopped outside a circus tent. From then the training began and we became circus stars. Until we decided we had to escape...

Emma Weir
Carrickfergus Grammar School, Carrickfergus

The Land Of Shroks

There was once a land of Shorks far, far away. Shrok was a green relative from Shrek. But there was one major problem with Shrokland. There were nasty purple Shroks. The Shroks were battling over each other's land and one green Shrok bit a purple Shrok, they were all annoyed by this and they all fought. Then came the biggest Shrok of them all, the Shork swallowed all the purple Shorks whole and they all cheered, 'Shrok! Shrok! Shrok!' The Shroks were so happy that they had a party for the biggest Shork. They all lived happily forever.

Bailey Mcalister (12)
Carrickfergus Grammar School, Carrickfergus

Caleb's Alien Encounter

'Caleb, wake-up, you need to get some bacon for breakfast,' screamed Eve.
Finished, now that's a perfectly knotted shoe! I left the house when I heard a bang! What was that... a wide, giant purple blob appeared in front of me.
'Argh!' I yelled at the top of my lungs. *Oh yes, I can use my electric brain power to kill the purple blob, Sizzle!* There goes the purple blob. Now where is the bacon in Superfields butcher? Oh there it is! Now let's pay for this and then head home before I see another blob...

Amye Louise Sleator (13)
Carrickfergus Grammar School, Carrickfergus

Under Our World

Wind rustling through her long frizzy hair, as she ran away from the orphanage. She hid by the sea and saw a strange and beautiful light. Suddenly she was transported to an underwater world. Here she could be with magical talking dolphins and violet turtles. This girl didn't have a home but neither did anyone else. In this beautiful land there was a wise queen who knew all. This little girl gathered up all her courage and asked where her parents were. Through a mirror she could see them looking for their little girl. She had a family...

Abi Crooks (12)
Carrickfergus Grammar School, Carrickfergus

Ungol, The Place Of War

Ungol was ruled by the high council. Well, the human inhabited regions were. The other regions were places no man dared go as they would quickly be slain by a massive beast. However, in recent years a new threat had arose. A huge threat... Orlags, twice the size of men with four times the strength. Their leader, Sarath, was a humanoid creature with coal-black skin, no mouth or nose and eyes of fire with long black pupils (similar to cat's eyes) which could pierce any man's soul. So far the high councils counter attacks had proven fruitless...

Robbie Taylor (13)
Carrickfergus Grammar School, Carrickfergus

Sidland

Night came at Hong King Zoo, and Owen the sloth was feeling tired. He gently dozed off to sleep, and found himself in a whole new world. He was amazed to see that he was surrounded by thousands of sloths, going about their human-like lives. Owen was confused as they were wearing clothes, and he was naked in the other sloth's eyes. He quickly realised this and ran as fast as he could to a clothes shop (not very fast as sloths are slow). He went into the shop and asked, 'Where am I?'
The shopkeeper replied, 'You're in Sidland.'

Adam McConnell (12)
Carrickfergus Grammar School, Carrickfergus

Candy Lane

Sophia was quietly walking past an old sweet shop window when suddenly, she saw something very tiny on her pink shoelaces. Sophia bent down and attended to this mysterious figure. It was a little girl dressed in sweetie wrappers from Celebrations. The little girl was called Strawb. Strawb came from a very yummy world called Candy Lane. She had come to this world to find someone to save their world as the evil king Dentose was trying to take over. So Strawb asked Sophia to follow her, though it was hard because she's very small! They came to a door...

Sarah Boyd (13)
Carrickfergus Grammar School, Carrickfergus

The World Inside You

If you close your eyes and think really hard, you can be transported to the world inside you. The little computer boy tried this once and he journeyed into this immense landscape. Digital emoticons instead of emotions, text bubbles instead of thoughts, for this was all that was behind those thick walls of glasses. The little girl also tried it and she travelled to a place where princesses trapped in the subconscious had happily ever afters. Though after you come out, well, you need imagination to go in, imagination will be gone. D'you want to?

Laura Madden (12)
Carrickfergus Grammar School, Carrickfergus

The Underground

They say you never see the bullet that gets you. That applied to when I first discovered the underground. I fell, the next thing I knew I was there. Firstly, I thought I was fine, before I noticed some odd details. The sky, not blue, white, no clouds in sight. After looking further, there were walls all around that went sky high, and no gates anywhere. Then, it hit me. I was underground. The sky was just mirrors, reflecting light from huge spotlights. The walls were earth. Buildings were dark and muddy and all people were very strange. Bizarre...

Reece William Stronge (14)
Carrickfergus Grammar School, Carrickfergus

Vodale

Everything was normal. Glamorous lights covered Vodale. Amy and Amber were about to get into their beds when suddenly they heard scattering and fear amongst people outside. They rushed over to their window in the corner of their room to see what was going on. They heard screaming as loud as you would scream watching horror movies. Amy and Amber were smart, they knew straight away that a bomb was let off and they were petrified. They ran down the stairs to find their mum in the car. They drove as fast as a cheetah, still feeling dreadfully frightened.

Megan Spence (12)
Carrickfergus Grammar School, Carrickfergus

Hell On Earth

What's Hell to you? To me it is what I'm ready for and every day life. I'm an Amedie. I'm ready for when Sirus and his blades bring hell to Earth. Sirus is the Devil and his blades are the demons he has possessed. It's happening, I'm ready. The skies are turning blood-red, the roads are cracking. It is the beginning of hell on Earth. I prepare for Sirus, wait for him to show himself.
The fight has begun. All I need to do is kill Sirus, then all his blades will be free.
With his back turned, *bam...*

Elizabeth Mary Hanna (13)
Carrickfergus Grammar School, Carrickfergus

The Lost World

Our story starts off on Earth with an intelligent scientist named Intel Igent. He finished creating a... teleporter! He used it immediately. Intel arrived somewhere new and opened the door to a face with sharp teeth staring at him angrily. A dinosaur! Intel quickly slid through the beast's legs and ran for safety in the forest. He set up camp and enjoyed everything until he saw a ball of lightning heading towards him. Thinking quickly, he ran for his teleporter, ignoring every huge beast. He stepped in, pressed the button... it didn't work!

Ryan Kennedy (12)
Carrickfergus Grammar School, Carrickfergus

Welcome To Hell

When someone thinks about Hell they think about fiery deaths. Home? A place where you feel comfortable? But what if I told you they were wrong? Hell.
Our home. We live there, with the guilt. We call night terrors. They live in your head and haunt you at night. They find your memories of loved ones and murder them in front of you. They will never break me, as I am the last optimist. At least that's what I thought until they reached my thoughts, everything I loved disappeared, every last glimpse of light is gone. I am the first sufferer.

Abbie Clarke
Carrickfergus Grammar School, Carrickfergus

The Land Above The Clouds

Clouds... Wonderful, wonderful clouds! What do you think is above them? Well, Sarah Field knows - it has pink grass and cotton candy trees. But it's not always happy here... sometimes, things go wrong. Sarah is playing with the squirrels and deer when she hears an unusual whirling sound. She turns round to face an old-aged, fair-skinned man with a beard as bushy as a squirrel's tail. He begins to cut down the pink trees and the world turns night and everything turns grey! Sarah has to chase him all across the island. Will she catch him?

Paige Pollock (12)
Carrickfergus Grammar School, Carrickfergus

Snake Tales

Oishee, Sassy, Rochedale, Jeremiah and JME, all survivors of a plane crash in a jungle in Vietnam. Everything went up in smoke apart from two guns and five rounds of ammo. The lads all trying to survive in a jungle full of mystery. The Vietnam tribes had traps set up everywhere. JME fell through a trap door into a snake pit. Further on into the night, screams and giggles from all directions, a witch chased Rochedale and killed him. Low on food, Sassy and Oishee decided to kill Jeremiah and eat him. In the end Oishee and Sassy became kings!

Cameron Long (14)
Carrickfergus Grammar School, Carrickfergus

Who Was He?

Everything had changed within him dramatically since the attacks. He barely recognised himself. Now he was completely under the control of the invaders. Had he been more alert in the early days he could have fled when he had the chance, but he'd hesitated and ended up being part of the first group to be rounded up by the invading troops. Betraying his friends and family had been easier than he thought it would be. The thought of what they might do to him if he went against them helped him sleep at night. What did he do to himself?

Caitlin MacManus (13)
Carrickfergus Grammar School, Carrickfergus

Cave Chaos!

'I finally found it!' shouted Jerry excitedly. The two men had come from the city of Sebula, a city with many different creatures and humans discovering more. If you found a new specimen, you would send it to Sebula to have examinations to find the species of organisms that you have found. Two of the members of Sebula previously found a map and now found the cave that the map had led them to. Jerry and Tom went inside. The walls were splat with violet and emerald. As they tiptoed through they suddenly saw glowing eyes. What could it be?

Jay MacQuarrie (13)
Carrickfergus Grammar School, Carrickfergus

The Democratic State Of Ezam

In 2004, several wealthy businessmen backed a small group of criminals in an attempt to overthrow the democracy and seize power for themselves. This was because Ezam has a healthy economy and is rich in natural resources and the grouping had intended to deprive the ordinary people of the standard of living expected on the island. Thankfully, the police and army received enough information from the population to enable the culprits to be arrested, tried and imprisoned for the attempted takeover, and life for Ezamers quickly returned to normal.

Madison Abigail Doyle (13)
Carrickfergus Grammar School, Carrickfergus

Dystopia

Sleep no longer came easily, like every other night I woke up to the sounds of gunshots and bombs. I moved my rags and stepped out of my bed, I looked to our new normality, war, screaming and crying. My colourless room offered nothing, we have no comfort. Gone were the days of retreat from the world. Sadly, I could hear my parents argue again. I no longer had a routine. Everyone lost track of time. I decided to escape on a scavenger hunt - anywhere was better than my old life in this old world, colourless. The world was ending.

Ruth Sarah McElveen (13)
Carrickfergus Grammar School, Carrickfergus

The Rebel

A man called James is working as a slave under a corrupt government. The year is 2400 and Mombek is a dystopian world with the dreaded slave keepers' robots who will stun slaves if they don't do their jobs. The man, named James, didn't work so a slave keeper stunned him but the robot overloaded and James escaped and ran to the control towers, he managed to get inside and shut the bots down. The slaves ran over the robots, making them explode. James was lifted into the sky and crowned as the hero of the new, safe Mombek.

Evan Higgins (12)
Carrickfergus Grammar School, Carrickfergus

Zara Knigtly's Legacy Of Oz

Zara thought back to the morning, she was with Oz the Great and Terrible. How her hand shook, her mind wavered. She had come a long way from then and there she was, fighting a battle against the Dark Wizard. Only light could harm dark and he was wicked, destroying Oz for a curse. Zara didn't think she could win this, but she remembered it was her legacy, being the one to save Oz. Zara pushed herself and her magic shot out in a purple light, defeating the Dark Wizard. 'I did it!' Zara was victorious. The battle was won.

Asha McClean (12)
Carrickfergus Grammar School, Carrickfergus

Escape To Zell-Am-See

The cold snow crunched as she dug her feet into the thick covering of frost on the mountain. The freezing air hit her quivering body and made her limbs numb. The trees whistled as the wind danced in and out of their branches. A single bird yelled its shrill call into the never-ending forest. She slipped into a dip and watched the moon crawl through the millions of stars; she glanced at her watch, which shimmered in the moon's light... and she smiled. As she lay in the freezing snow, her head began to clear and finally... she was free.

Sarah Brown
Carrickfergus Grammar School, Carrickfergus

The Danger Zone

She's gone, but still here. I know how to get her back. I have to read, the book. 'The Danger Zone' by Kristen Moore. Suddenly, I was transported to an unfamiliar place. It was dark and cold. I realised I was in the danger zone. 'Leah!' I cried. No answer. I felt something whizz past my head and turned to see an arrow in a tree. I ran until I found Leah. 'We have to go?' I begged.
'You can't,' said a figure as it pulled out a gun. I got Leah's gun and shot the figure. We were home!

Kristen Moore (12)
Carrickfergus Grammar School, Carrickfergus

Home

I could see them coming from however far away they were. They circled us. They poked us. They made fools of us! I could see new colours. What they called green, blue and red. It was beautiful. We knew we had found a good home. The humans, as they had decided to be called, were relatively welcoming. However, the air seemed a bit dark for our liking. But, home is home. We decided that we could change to look like them, but they feared we were too powerful. They underestimated our power when they attacked us. Now we rule Earth.

Finlay A Rogan (14)
Carrickfergus Grammar School, Carrickfergus

The Atlantic Kingdom

Far beneath the ocean there was a fish called Singa who was only born one month ago. Singa was learning fast, he lived in an extraordinary place with lots to do and had a brother to keep him company. When Singa was four he could walk, talk, read and write. It was easier to teach fish than humans because fish were more intelligent. Singa was six when he was ready for scaole (fish school). Singa was quite nervous because he was a late starter at school and wasn't ready to take on the new challenges that lay ahead in life.

Jake Corbett (12)
Carrickfergus Grammar School, Carrickfergus

The Runner

It was chaos outside. Screams ran through the town as people attacked each other, not knowing whether they were the monsters or not. Mum and Dad had boarded up the windows and doors of the house, while they got me and John to grab any things that could be used as a weapon and put them in our school bags. *Crash!* 'They got in!' said Dad. 'Heather, take the boys and get out of here. I'll hold them off as long as I can. Go!' My mum grabbed me and John and we ran. My dad screaming as we went...

Lloyd Cole (13)
Carrickfergus Grammar School, Carrickfergus

Lonely Ice Island

Ice and ice, the only thing in sight, the clear white ice which shouldn't exist, in fact, none of this should be here even the... uh-oh, here they come, the tiny vicious squirrels coming for me or the food which is the only source of food. They aren't a problem, if my pals, the mammoths, arrive and kick the squirrels out of existence, it should be OK. This world I'm in is a world where the land is flat and a never-ending loop of ice. I come to clear my mind to relax in this quiet land, my lonely land.

Rhys Pennell (12)
Carrickfergus Grammar School, Carrickfergus

The Murder

Normal days failed to exist ever since she met him. Her days were filled with sadness and fear. What if he returned? Would he finally finish what he started? Every time the phone rang, or someone knocked at her door, her heart raced. She hadn't left her flat in six months. Today was not a normal day, it was stranger than usual. She felt as though she was being watched, as if she wasn't alone. She searched the flat, no one was there. Just as she sat down, he burst through the door. This time, she knew he would kill her.

Aimee McCartan (13)
Carrickfergus Grammar School, Carrickfergus

Portal To Portania

I bolt. Not looking behind me. I stop. Standing in front of me is a purple, glowing portal that throbs very quickly. I dash rapidly towards it. I gaze in surprise at this unusual find. I get sucked in. I find myself slowly losing control of my body. I am spinning. I drop. I have now entered this strange land, confused and scared. Around me are pot holes of lava everywhere. I anxiously step towards a building close by. I keep focused. I am nervous. I all of a sudden feel heat beneath me. I slip, beneath me is... 'Argh!'

Grace Delucchi (12)
Carrickfergus Grammar School, Carrickfergus

The Secret Sea

Splash! I had fallen into the icy-cold water. I sank to the bottom of the deep sea but I could still breathe normally. The sign said: 'Mystical Marine Bay'. I was so confused. As I swam closer, I saw iridescent colours and vibrant fish. Mermaids were swimming past my face. *I knew they were real!* I thought to myself. I saw a coral castle, so I immediately thought that there was a king or queen of this realm. As I swam closer it went blurry. I could not see! I woke up in my bed with a huge bruise.

Nicola Smyth (12)
Carrickfergus Grammar School, Carrickfergus

The Cursed Island

Urgh! Another day in Horn Bay. Lonely and isolated with nobody to talk to, a girl sits leaning against a palm tree. She breathes in the fresh sea breeze and takes in the breathtaking view of clear blue seas and scorching hot sun. As the young girl rose to her feet, a group of strange creatures appear. Some have long necks and fluffy tails, others have large wings. She begins pushing the creatures with fins out to sea and gasps as they pass through the barrier and she follows as they have broken the enchanted curse!

Jessica Hayes (12)
Carrickfergus Grammar School, Carrickfergus

Trapped

I woke up, I couldn't open my eyes, feel my legs or I couldn't move an inch. There were people standing over me but I couldn't make out who these odd-looking characters were. I wasn't able to speak and these people put something over the top of my head. One of them was standing over my paralysed body with a Kindle Fire HD typing stuff into it. They brought another person but this time it was a woman and they did exactly the same tests. While they were taking the test there was a loud bang, was help coming?

Reuben Baker
Carrickfergus Grammar School, Carrickfergus

Apocalypse Rising

It was the first nuclear war. North Korea were the first people to send a missile, it was no normal missile it was a missile that could turn a whole country into zombies in less than ten seconds. My brother and I were home alone, we just about made it to the bomb shelter. We also brought my granda's shotgun.

Two days later, we went back up to the surface. We saw weird monsters crawling around. We needed food and supplies. My brother and I got to the house then we saw a helicopter. It was there to help us!

Joshua Strudwick (13)
Carrickfergus Grammar School, Carrickfergus

The Unspoken Island

I was chilling on my island, like I usually do, with all my unspoken of mysterious animals. Animals that have never been imagined by any human on Earth and it was to stay this way. But on this random day, in the distance, I saw three pirate ships approaching land. All the mysterious animals and I panicked. We knew this day was going to come, but not so soon. I declared to all the animals to calm down and prepare for battle, as we all knew this day was to come. We got to battle positions and prepared.

Lewis Elmes (14)
Carrickfergus Grammar School, Carrickfergus

Earth 2.0

Once upon a time in the far-off future, there lived a boy called John. He lived on a fabulous new planet called Earth 2.0, but all was not as peaceful as you would think - a new ruler had just risen to power and had locked all the world's inhabitants in one big city. But, one day an earthquake shook the city to its centre. This was actually a blessing in disguise as the earthquake had knocked down a section of the wall. It was then that John and Mark and Evan made their escape and went back to Earth.

Alex Millar (12)
Carrickfergus Grammar School, Carrickfergus

The Dark Room

As I walked towards the door it creaked open. My stomach was turning. No light shone through the small space between the door and the wall. I pushed the door until the whole room was in my sight. It was a pitch-black room with no light except a door at the end of the room. It was like a white sun. As I walked towards it, it didn't get any bigger or smaller. It was like I wasn't moving at all.
After a while the door was getting bigger. Although I couldn't see out of it, it got bigger...

Lara Ellerslie
Carrickfergus Grammar School, Carrickfergus

False Reality

As I drift off to sleep I think of a world much different than mine. One where everybody says hi to a passerby, one with kindness, one with no violence, one where people respect others' religions, but most of all a world with peace. But in reality, the world is a much different place than my dream one. It is a place with little kindness, a place engulfed in violence and I don't think that is going to change, not in my lifetime anyway. So I guess for now I can only dream of a world of peace.

Jack Campbell (13)
Carrickfergus Grammar School, Carrickfergus

One More Day

Another day in Desert Valley. Food and water are scarce, I must find someone to steal from, but I must be careful out there. If a savage spots me I'm dead, they kill without a second thought, that's what happened to the rest of my family, even the children. Maybe I can find someone to team with, work together to survive in this hell-ridden world, but until then I'll stay low, stay quiet. If I'm lucky I might just survive and make it one more day.

Jonathan Geoff Graham (14)
Carrickfergus Grammar School, Carrickfergus

The War That Changed Everything

John was wandering around in his garden then he saw something like a bomb.
He was the only person that didn't know about the nuclear war. *Bang! Bang!* Bombs were dropping everywhere.
Two hundred years later the war ended, everyone died except those that were prepared. People arose but they weren't people anymore, they were robots and they weren't on earth anymore! The world moved closer to the moon and the robots floated across. Suddenly, *boom!* The earth exploded. The robots had to find shelter before the meteor shower. Luckily they found shelter but they were confused about what happened...

Callum Squair (11)
Elgin High School, New Elgin

The Witch's Challenge

Outside a town called Elgin, Edith was practising her magic in the Linkwood Burn.
She started chanting an odd string of words. Edith saw an explosion out of the corner of her eye, 'What now?' she said and she ran home. Her BFF, Bradley, joined her as she ran, and explained what happened.
'Your parents blew up Tesco,' he panted.
'I'm glad I'm not like my parents!' replied Edith, as she cast a shield charm over everyone.
'What are you doing?' yelled her mother. 'If you don't start acting like a witch, we're going to put you to the test...'

Abbie Howie (11)
Elgin High School, New Elgin

It's You

'Leave me alone please,' Ava screamed from the inside of her wardrobe. It was very dark and something uninvited had came into her house. A huge beast with large horns and jagged teeth was lurking around waiting for Ava.
Ava crept out of the wardrobe and took a peep through the window. Monsters everywhere! 'I'm so confused,' Ava stuttered. She felt a cold, rough arm grab her shoulder.
'Do you want to know something?' the monster said. 'You're the only human left so actually you're the strange one. We're all normal and it's time for that to change.

Alana Marie Wall (12)
Elgin High School, New Elgin

Control

'What's happening to me?' said Lana.
'You're the second person to have powers like me,' said Dave.
'But I'm scared, I can't do this!' shouted Lana, who was now twenty feet in the air.
'Yes you can! You have to learn to control it!' shouted Dave.
'But how?' screamed Lana, constantly floating upwards.
'Control your emotions, calm down and you will start to come back down,' said Dave. Then she started to come back down, it was a relief for Dave because he thought she was going to keep on going up and up out of sight...

Jennifer McBride (11)
Elgin High School, New Elgin

Stagelight

I'm here on the stage. The stage lights are shining in my eyes. I can hear people but I can't see them, all I can see is the stage light and these dark shapes moving round. I thought that it was just my nerves getting to me. Suddenly, the talking and shouting stop. I start to shout, 'Hello, is anyone there?' but no one replied. Suddenly, the stage lights start to flicker. I am scared. I suddenly feel an ice-cold breeze, then it stops again. I need help and fast. The breeze starts again. Who is there and why?

Emillie Dean (12)
Elgin High School, New Elgin

The Alien's Lost Key

It was a normal day on the moon. The streets were filled with aliens. The houses were empty as most aliens were on holiday to Mars. The Wubble family were coming back from the shop when they realised that they lost the house key. They decided to go through and live in their neighbours house cause they were on holiday. But the neighbour's spaceship just landed on the moon. When the neighbours arrived home they phoned the police on the Wubbles. The neighbours said they would lock their door from then on so that they were kept safe.

Eve Campbell (12)
Elgin High School, New Elgin

The Apocalypse

He kicked down the door in hope that there were more people. He checked all the rubble but didn't find anyone. Tom started to panic until he heard some noises. He thought he'd found civilisation but then he heard a strange sound coming from underneath the ground. He turned around and noticed something coming out of the ground. It was a pair of arms. He looked around and there they were: the zombies. He climbed on top of a big rock and shouted for help.

He tried to fend them off but there were too many. It was too late.

Ben Grant (12)
Elgin High School, New Elgin

The Planet Of Doom

In the future, in space, in the year 2030, there is going to be an unknown planet with thousands of aliens living there. One sunny day it will begin to get extremely hot and the aliens, who will originally be green, will start to turn red because of the heat.

One day, it will get so hot that burning meteorites will fall onto the planet. The planet will start to turn red-hot and lava pits will form and everything will burn away. Eventually it will get too hot for the aliens to handle and they will possibly die away.

Katie Louise Mighten (12)
Elgin High School, New Elgin

The Lockdown

I was running down the dark corridor of Chicago High School. I was scared for my life. There were five men following me and my two friends down the corridor. They were armed with guns, knives and all other kinds of weapons.

I was thinking they could be here for revenge for when we sent horse worms to try and take over their country. We ran past Miss Campbell's classroom.

All of the younger children had been sent to hide under desks and in cupboards. This was such a disaster. I will never forget this day...

Olivia Eve Ravenscroft (12)
Elgin High School, New Elgin

Two Worlds At War

Another day in Central London, World War Two. As I awoke from my dreamless sleep I heard a strange noise from the inside of my crooked wardrobe. I stood up for a closer look. It began dragging me in forcefully towards the open doors. A blinding light shone through the doors.
I woke up in a strangely soft bed, stood up and looked out of the window to toadstools and flowers as far as the eye could see. I heard gunfire and ear-splitting bangs and found the same wardrobe at the other side of the room. I ran for it...

Emma-Jayne Russell (12)
Elgin High School, New Elgin

This Is My Life

My name is Lily. I'm eleven and one of the few survivors of one of the worst wars future Earth has seen. I hope your world is nothing like mine, every day you hear gunshots, every day someone screams, every day is a misery.
You're lucky. This is the great war, there are ten survivors. We thrive, preferring to survive. Nine people are adults, I am the only child survivor. I am only a child. I can survive, I am going to finish what my father started. My name is Lilly B. Ray, one of the few survivors...

Kaitlin Duggan (11)
Elgin High School, New Elgin

The Magical Sword

Once upon a time there was a land of sick animals and one little starving family with a magical sword, but they didn't know it was magical. They needed to eat so they went out to kill the animals for food. They hunted one animal but it healed it. They didn't understand. Then they tried to kill the same animal when it was healed but nothing happened. So they got another sword and killed another animal normally. They then all went home and cooked their steak burgers and enjoyed the rest of their night.

Ann-Mairi Stevenson (11)
Elgin High School, New Elgin

Dearth Clan

On 1817, June the 17th, at 11pm, I was looking at my telescope when I saw a planter pop up, it made Mars fly into a million pieces. So I called Pilot Systems to check it out. We went to the planet.
When we made it to the planet he landed the rocket. Once we got out the rocket it blew up. We'd landed on a massive landscape filled with lava. We saw the Dearth Clan. The creature who ruled the planet killed 57 people with his minions. He killed the rest of us and then destroyed Earth and was happy.

Kian Stanford (12)
Elgin High School, New Elgin

Alien Land

The aliens are trying to take over the world. They are nearly finished planning and there are just a few more aliens to come and join them. They have got all their tools and their spaceships. After all that, they are finished, so they finally start. So they start coming from underground. Then they start killing people. Then they realise that they are in the wrong place and there are police with guns. Soon it ends in a epic failure and they all get killed. All that they did was a waste of time.

Cameron Donaldson (12)
Elgin High School, New Elgin

She Is Real

It is a nice night and Kenzi was reading a book about the queen, he thought she wasn't real.
The next morning he went for a walk in the woods and he found a path, so he followed it. He got to the top and he didn't know where he was so he looked around. He found a castle and wanted to look around in it, so he did. Halfway round he found a big room and in it was the queen. *She is actually real,* he thought. He rushed home in excitement and told his mum and dad.

Amy Leigh Taylor (11)
Elgin High School, New Elgin

The Ultra Space

I have to. I have to leave. I look into the empty hole that is the portal. I have to go, I look around. The palm trees sway in the wind, the ocean waves in the setting sun. I look into the portal. I step in. My bracelet starts to glow. It is so dark I can barely see. I look into the distance. It isn't just darkness, I can see odd-looking trees. They grow down from above but there is no visible roof.
And that is not all; I can see an odd jelly fish like creature. Strange...

Tyler-James Green (12)
Elgin High School, New Elgin

The Discovery Of A Lifetime!

The shuttle door opened as commander Cay-9 slowly trembled down the ramp as he just arrived on the undiscovered bizarre planet of Topak. The dusty ground was red and the sun grew over the horizon as he set foot on Topak. Just as he looked up, he heard a loud bang and the sound of vehicles. He was not sure what to do, whether to run or to stay, would they be friendly or would they attack? He got his gun off his back and was ready to fire when he heard the sound of bullets and ran.

Aidan Roger (11)
Elgin High School, New Elgin

Haunted

One dark and stormy night, two boys went to an abandoned house in a weird alleyway. One of the boys knew that it was haunted and left the other boy alone. He went home and the other boy never came back. The boy who knew it was haunted felt really bad, he thought that his friend had died. The next day the police and the neighbourhood went out looking for him. Later that day the police had found him but he was dead. His family and friends were so sad.

Lauren Davies (11)
Elgin High School, New Elgin

The End

We emerged from the apartment. 'A-a-are you sure about this?' staggered Max, as we advanced into the war-riddled city. It was like the purge, empty streets with icy-cold shrieks sending shivers down your spine, followed by the crackle of a gunshot, or the shatter of glass after grenades or intricate home-made bombs were detonated. Although we were heavily armed and protected, our goal was to help the injured or wounded and bring the deceased back to their families, and overall bring an end to this pointless conflict. Suddenly, a grenade was launched at us: was this the end?

Ross Allan (13)
Mackie Academy, Stonehaven

The War Is Over

The war was finally over, although it had been at least two years, it looked exactly the same; it was as if the war was just yesterday. Everyone in our small town was either fighting over how things should be done, or trying to get our home back together again.
Soon after the war, we became a dictatorship because the war started after people were constantly at battle. There was arguing, even threatening their neighbours.
After months of fighting, it just exalted, and that's when everyone started to ruin buildings. Nothing was left, however nobody talks about that anymore.

Molly Brown (12)
Mackie Academy, Stonehaven

The Void

Khan was boarding the great Owken ship; he was discovering beyond the reach of Sol, taking back the reach of their previous planets that were washed away by The Void. The Owken ships where powered by an ancient civilisation's core planet who were ironically named the Owken, he boarded the ship.
Weeks passed and they found the planet they were looking for in the vast regions of space. He got his spacesuit on and went out onto the planet and explored. He found nothing then screamed as a strange blue substance came out of the ground... The Void...

Cameron Goodall Duncan (13)
Mackie Academy, Stonehaven

Rollington

Rollington was a place where problems weren't heard of. A boy, named Bob Washington, lived there with his family. Bob arrived at school that day to find that school was closed and there was a note on the door saying: 'Hide!'
Rollington had a secret that nobody knew about, they had a volcano which used to be active but nobody had heard from it in ages. The reason the school was closed was because the volcano had erupted on the other side of town and everyone was hiding. Bob's parents made him hide, they didn't want him getting hurt.

Jack Beattie (12)
Mackie Academy, Stonehaven

Rebellion

I stare at the people around me in the sterile white room. Hushed whispers echo through the space, talk of rebellion and freedom. I don't know why they bother. The gleaming cameras loom from every corner of the room - the rebels won't last long. Everyone knows the consequence of revolting.
I look down at the bowl of mush in my hands and sigh. It's just another way to control us - make us eat the same disgusting food; make us 'enjoy' meals at the same time every day.
I force down another repulsive mouthful - and that's when the screaming starts...

Helena Rendall (12)
Mackie Academy, Stonehaven

How The Germans Took Over The World

A war has started between the Germans and the east side of the world. Everyone's terrified of who is going to make the first move. Germany invades Poland. The UK and France declare war on Germany initiating WWII in Europe. Couple of years later... 'News just came in that Nazi Germany has invented a nuclear bomb and might be using it to bomb us and America.'

Couple of days later... 'The Germans just launched the first ever nuke at the UK and possibly America, we'll wait to see the amount of confirmed deaths and that's all for the news.'

Aaron Henry (12)
Mackie Academy, Stonehaven

It All Started

Before it all happened we were happy under one ruler, suddenly the king mysteriously died and the kingdom was left to his two sons. They fought for months over the kingdom and fighting broke into war. Scotary had split in half, the Davies against the Simpas, just ordinary people fighting for a king.

They made their own huts because everything had been destroyed, they farmed for food and traded with others to survive, people did what they wanted because Scotary was lawless and every day at 12pm they would fight to the death, people were dropping like flies.

Abbey Lindsay (13)
Mackie Academy, Stonehaven

Kidnapping

The dark sky around me drives shivers up my spine, along with the faint frightful sounds of the night. As I'm coming home I walk on the pavement and the road is silent, which is frightening considering there's always something mischievous in our rebellious world.
As I walk I hear something drive along the road. I turned my head round to see what it is; it was a large van with some spray painting on the side. Someone opens the door and reaches out to grab me. Two men jump out and start to sprint, chasing me down the street...

Ellie Katy Smith (13)
Mackie Academy, Stonehaven

A Horrible/Happy Day

Five years ago today the world was destroyed, everyone was very unhappy. We had a leader that we don't speak about because he was the worst. When our leader died we needed a new one. After months we finally got one, he came and ruled our world but he was the worst. He started wars and clans and you had to obey him or you would get punished.

Now our world is very different because the leader died five years ago today. So we have a new leader. She stopped all the fighting and destroyed the clans, now everyone gets along.

Lucy Henry (12)
Mackie Academy, Stonehaven

Trump's Invasion

I was in China the day the bombs dropped but luckily I survived. I went to scour the streets for survivors but I looked for hours but nothing apart from corpses upon corpses. Then the troops stormed China and Russia on boats, helicopters and cars. They started searching down through the streets. I was spotted by one of the troops. I had to do something so I grabbed a brick from one of many fallen structures and *bang*, right over his head. I ran to him, grabbed his gun and ran far away up into the woods to camp out.

Richie Henderson (13)
Mackie Academy, Stonehaven

Sweet Dreams

I should never have watched that movie before bed, every time I tried to close my eyes all I could see was green, flesh-eating zombies with bones missing and blood oozing down their eyes. I was guessing it was night because it was dark and silent, except the evil-spirited zombies mumbling words I couldn't understand. They were walking closer to me, ten zombies against one girl who was tiny to them. I closed my eyes and then opened them, hoping it was a dream and that I was just in my bed, but it wasn't...

Marci-Beth Pyper Robertson (12)
Mackie Academy, Stonehaven

Atlanta City

The city of Atlanta is a place of beauty to all. The city attracted rich people like moths to a lamp. But there was one man, Richard Collins, who had been really rich, but lost it all after his bank went into debt. He hadn't paid the huge tax that citizens had to pay, and he was in trouble. When police came knocking on his door he knew it spelt trouble. He grabbed his emergency bag and headed for the window. He leapt out and headed away from the street of towering mansions and away from the city he knew.

Samuel William McFarland (13)
Mackie Academy, Stonehaven

All I Remember

All I remember is that I was at Swenarc Park and I saw a big, scary figure. Now I'm in a bed that I don't know. I look in the mirror and I barely recognise myself, my hair is short and died black, my face is covered in freckles and I'm wearing thick glasses. I get up to look around but nothing here is mine. I open the bedroom door...
'Where are you going honey?' I glance round quickly seeing a man in 'my' bed.
And then it clicks, the person in my bed was the figure at the park...

Cara Davie (12)
Mackie Academy, Stonehaven

Geef

I am the oldest creature on Geef. I am precisely 120 years and 360 days old. Geef used to be such a nice place to live, a leaf in Scotland, a bit cold but never the less beautiful. I remember the days before pollution lined the sky, when the world was beautiful, when we thought Planet Earth would never end. Now though the humans have ruined the place, with their fancy cars and huge factories. They've made it so hard to live and breathe. Now Geef is about to die, the world is about to end because of them.

Mairi Elizabeth Wilson (13)
Mackie Academy, Stonehaven

Banker In The Life Of Crime

As you come past the town hall you see all the windows and broken doors with spray paint on them, that's why we live like animals. I used to work for the bank I was Chief Banker but we got robbed soon after the country lost their heads. I was robbed six times but the police gave up after the third time. This showed that the entire country had given up. I have turned to a life of crime, I steal food for my family and I live in a place with a corrugated roof on four sticks...

Stuart Burr (13)
Mackie Academy, Stonehaven

The Life On Zembee!

The worlds of people are getting evacuated. My son, he has gone without me. He's in one of the spaceships. I've been left behind on Zembee. I'm all by myself because the planets are about to collide with dangerous and low oxygen. I'm stuck under a massive stone. The planet has taken all my fresh air. A man has got an oxygen mask on and another is on the way for me. I'm safe, he has put the oxygen mask on me. We find a spaceship, we are off now to find my son on Earth.

Nikkitta-Marie Julie Clark (12)
Mackie Academy, Stonehaven

The Ruler

I look around and see a huge desk with a huge chair at it. Sitting on the chair is a man and sitting on the table is piles of paperwork. This man is the ruler of our world, Asisia. I am the long-lost cousin of this man, the long-lost cousin of our ruler. I look around some more and see a small wooden box. He must see me looking at it curiously because he stands from his chair, walks over to the box and opens up the lid. Inside is a strange planet he calls Earth.

Ellen Thomson (12)
Mackie Academy, Stonehaven

Untitled

Hi, my name is Penny and I am a Pufferfish. I live in Pescalonia. It is an underwater land. When the sun shines into the water it lights up the underwater plants and rocks in a bright and colourful way. However, when the sun doesn't shine it's a dark, gloomy and scary place.
Carly the crab and I were dressed for the disco. We danced the night away. Then disaster struck. Scar was on the prowl. The whole dance floor disappeared into the shark's vast jaws. We escaped by the skin of our teeth. It's a dangerous world in Pescalonia.

Rebecca-Jane Browne (14)
St Brigid's College, Shantallow

The Magical Girl

Once there was a girl named Emma. She was fifteen years old with brown hair, but there was a secret that no one knew: she and her twin sister, Lily, had magical powers. When they were upset they'd go to this world, named Sugar, with everything in it so perfect and sweet.
One day, it went really evil. The girls didn't know how it had happened but there was a person controlling the land so all the little animals and girls were doom and gloom. Emma found out that the evil lord was her own sister, she was worried...

Sarah Ramsey (14)
St Brigid's College, Shantallow

The Unexplaining

There was me and my friend, Harry, we went through a door and when we got through, the door slammed shut and locked on us. When we went down these steps we got to the bottom, it was cold and icy. We were lost in this unexplained world. Suddenly, we saw this monkey! His name was Steve. He helped us for a bit but he set us up and he took us to a place with his friend. They tried to kill us so we ran and shouted, 'Help!' We then ran back to the door and it opened...

Darren O'Donnell (14)
St Brigid's College, Shantallow

Sacturn

I live in the woods and in the woods there are diamonds buried there. I really need to get them to make some money but they are being watched by some monkeys. They have got some guns, the only way I'm getting them is hiring an army with guns and tanks. So I get an army and they help me. We get set up and we drive in. We start shooting and we take them all out. I see this gleaming shine. We go over and I get the diamonds. I am very happy!

Peter Rodgers (14)
St Brigid's College, Shantallow

YoungWriters
Est.1991

YOUNG WRITERS INFORMATION

We hope you have enjoyed reading this book – and that you will continue to in the coming years.

If you're a young writer who enjoys reading and creative writing, or the parent of an enthusiastic poet or story writer, do visit our website www.youngwriters.co.uk. Here you will find free competitions, workshops and games, as well as recommended reads, a poetry glossary and our blog.

If you would like to order further copies of this book, or any of our other titles, then please give us a call or visit www.youngwriters.co.uk.

Young Writers
Remus House
Coltsfoot Drive
Peterborough
PE2 9BF
(01733) 890066
info@youngwriters.co.uk